For my Jamesie – S.H.

Dedicated to my (not so) little brother Sheriph Adeola, I'm very proud of the father you've become and the brother you are. Love you dude. – D.A.

First published 2020 by Macmillan Children's Books
an imprint of Pan Macmillan
The Smithson, 6 Briset Street
London EC1M 5NR
Associated companies throughout the world
www.panmacmillan.com

ISBN (HB): 978-1-5290-1396-2
ISBN (PB): 978-1-5290-1397-9
ISBN (Ebook): 978-1-5290-4850-6

Text copyright © Swapna Haddow 2020
Illustrations copyright © Dapo Adeola 2020

The rights of Swapna Haddow and Dapo Adeola to be identified as
the author and illustrator of this work have been asserted by them
in accordance with the Copyright, Designs and Patents Act 1988.

9 8 7 6 5 4 3 2 1

A CIP catalogue record for this book is
available from the British Library.

Printed in China

Written by
SWAPNA HADDOW

Illustrated by
DAPO ADEOLA

MY DAD IS A GRIZZLY BEAR

MACMILLAN CHILDREN'S BOOKS

Shhh.
Beware.

My dad is a **grizzly bear.**

He has the fuzziest fur that **scratches** and **scritches.**

Mum laughs and teases him when he gives her big sloppy kisses.

He chases me and my sister, growling and waving his enormous paws, because he is a **grizzly bear.**

He eats all the honey in the house. It drips off his crumpets and sticks to his whiskers.

Drip.

Drip.

Driiiiiiip.

He never leaves any for me because he is a **grizzly bear.**

He naps all the time, anywhere, any place, day or night - in the car, in the pool, in the playground and even in the cinema.

Especially in the cinema.

ZZZ^Z

Sometimes he's asleep,
even when he's awake.

"Are you asleep, Dad?"

"Yes."

When he does wake up, he's so grumpy.
He **grumbles** and **grunts** and **stomps** around,
hunting for food, because he is a **grizzly bear.**

Sometimes at the weekend Dad makes the whole family go for loooooong walks in the woods, even when our legs are aching and our noses are frozen.

He's never cold because of all his thick **grizzly bear** fur.

Sometimes he catches fish in his **TEETH.**

Sometimes he climbs to the top of the **TALLEST** tree.

Sometimes he can run **FASTER** than a bus.

And he has the **LOUDEST** growl.

All because he is a **grizzly bear.**

One day, Dad packed
up the car and said,

"We're going Camping in the woods."

I hate camping.
The food is always soggy.
We always get lost.

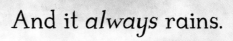

And it *always* rains.

We had to eat our wet, mushy
sandwiches under a tree while
Dad set up our tent.

Dad was very happy, because he is
a wood-dwelling **grizzly bear.**

At bedtime, Dad went for a wander in the woods, perhaps he was looking for his friends. Mum tried to cheer us up with a story.

It was all about . . .

a **grizzly bear.**

A **huge** grizzly bear.
A huge, **hairy,** very scary,
grizzly bear.

A GIGANTIC, TERRIFYING, HUNGRY, VERY HUNGRY, OH SO HUNGRY GRIZZLY BEAR...

Maybe my Dad is
a bit **grumpy,**
and a bit **fuzzy.**

Maybe he does
eat all the honey.

And maybe he
would rather live
in the woods.

But when I'm scared,
there isn't anyone else
who can give me . . .

...the biggest, **warmest,** best ever

BEAR HUG!

My Dad may be a **grizzly bear**,
but he's my favourite **grizzly bear**.
Besides, there are fiercer
things than bears . . .

Wait until you hear my Mum
ROAR!